★ SPORTS STARS ★

RAMON MARTINEZ
MASTER OF THE MOUND

BY MARK STEWART

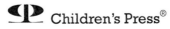

Children's Press®
A Division of Grolier Publishing
New York London Hong Kong Sydney
Danbury, Connecticut

Photo Credits

©: Allsport USA: 35 (Simon P. Barnett); AP Photo/file: 19; AP Photo/Kevork Djansezian: 18; AP/Wide World Photos: 31, 38, 39, 45 right; Best Cards, Birmingham, AL: 27; John Klein: 40; Pat Berrett: 22; Ron Vesely: 13, 14, 33; SportsChrome: 6, 28, 32, 44 right, 45 left, 46, 47 (Jeff Carlick), 21, 43 (Louis A. Raynor), 25, 44 left (C. Rydlewski); Tom Dipace: cover, 3, 9, 16, 37, 41.

Map by Mapping Specialists.

Library of Congress Cataloging-in-Publication Data

Stewart, Mark
    Ramon Martinez: master of the mound/ by Mark Stewart.
      p. cm. — (Sports stars)
    Summary: A biography of the young power pitcher for the Los Angeles Dodgers.
    ISBN 0-516-20699-0 (lib. bdg.) ISBN 0-516-26191-6 (pbk.)
    1. Martinez, Ramon, 1968- —Juvenile literature. 2. Baseball players—United States—Biography—Juvenile literature. 3. Baseball players—Dominican Republic—Biography—Juvenile literature. 4. Los Angeles Dodgers (Baseball team)— Juvenile literature.
    [1. Martinez, Ramon, 1968- . 2. Baseball players.] I. Title. II. Series.
GV 865.M356S84   1997
796.357'092   96–40434
[B]—DC21   CIP
                                          AC

CONTENTS

POWER AND PRECISION

A t Dodger Stadium, a batter steps into the batter's box and taps home plate with his bat. Dodgers pitcher Ramon Martinez stands on the mound and waits. The catcher puts down one finger, and Martinez nods his head in agreement. He rocks back and begins his motion. Drawing the ball out of the glove, Martinez twists his body like a coiled spring. Suddenly he snaps his arm forward and fires the ball toward home plate. The batter loses sight of the ball against Martinez's white uniform. As he tries to readjust, the ball hisses by him and explodes into the catcher's mitt. *Strike Three!* calls the umpire.

The catcher throws the ball triumphantly to the third baseman as the batter walks back to the dugout. He does not look forward to facing Martinez again.

At the beginning of his career, Ramon Martinez used power and pinpoint precision to strike out hitters. But arm fatigue and control difficulties reduced him to a shadow of his former self. After being booed off the mound at Dodger Stadium, he returned to throw a no-hitter. A true champion, he has battled back to regain his rightful position as pitching ace of the Los Angeles Dodgers.

Ramon has proved that he has the heart of a champion.

2

CHILDHOOD IN THE
DOMINICAN REPUBLIC

The Dominican Republic makes up the eastern two-thirds of the Caribbean island of Hispaniola. The nation's major industry is tourism; its most important exports include sugar, coffee, cocoa, and tobacco. It is a Spanish-speaking country of more than seven million people—and practically everyone is crazy for baseball.

Ramon Martinez grew up in the Mano Guayabo section of Santo Domingo, the country's capital and largest city. Like most boys in his neighborhood, he played a lot of baseball. Ramon learned the game on vacant lots and crude fields

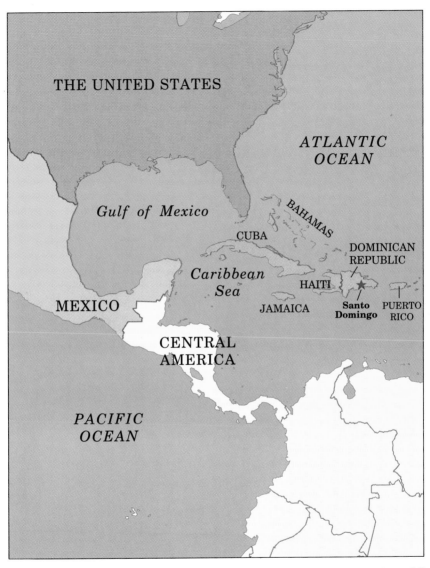

Ramon was born and raised in Santo Domingo, Dominican Republic.

along with his brothers, Nelson, Pedro, and Jesus. They used rubber balls and broom handles, and dreamed of someday becoming good enough to play in one of the many stadiums that dot the island. "We played baseball all the time," says Ramon, "in the streets, or wherever. I grew up this way. I was always active, playing with my friends, playing in parks that weren't in very good condition."

The Martinez family was very poor, and there was not always enough food for six growing children. There were eight people living in one small house that did not even have a toilet. Ramon's father, Paulino Jaime, worked hard as a school janitor. He expected his children to work just as hard—both on the field and in the classroom. Paulino had been a top amateur pitcher in his day, and he taught his sons his famous curveball. "A lot of people told me how good he was," says Ramon. "That made me want to play and to be somebody famous."

Ramon learned to pitch from both his father and on the streets
on Santo Domingo.

Although he has gained weight in the past few years, Ramon still looks skinny on the mound.

Ramon did not like to swing the bat or chase down balls in the field. And he had no interest in being a shortstop, which is considered the "glamour" position by most kids in the Dominican Republic. Ramon wanted to pitch.

He had an awkward motion that enabled him to "sling" the ball in such a way that batters had a hard time picking it up. His arms and legs all

seemed to be going in different directions.
He made quite a sight on the mound. At the age
of 15, Ramon was already more than 6 feet tall,
but he was desperately skinny, weighing barely
100 pounds!

One day, Ramon attended a special tryout for
the Los Angeles Dodgers. There, the reed-thin
teenager caught the eye of Ralph Avila, an
important person in Dominican baseball. Avila
invited Ramon to attend the Dodgers' Campo Las
Palmas baseball academy. A few days later,
Ramon arrived at Campos Las Palmas with a
torn baseball cap, a ragged glove, and no socks.
But he had something the other kids lacked—a
plan. "I wanted to get better every day," explains
Ramon. "I love to be first. I don't ever like to be
behind in anything. I have always been like this
since I began playing baseball."

For the first time in his life, Ramon was
provided with good equipment and playing
conditions at Campo Las Palmas. He already

knew how to throw—his fastball was decent and he could make the ball curve, too—but at the academy, he was taught how to pitch. "Location is everything," he remembers learning. "It's not how hard you throw it, it's where you throw it. You pitch to where the batter has the least balance."

From the academy, Ramon joined the local team in Mano Guayabo, the Braves. Ramon made an incredible 51 starts for the team that season, and he established himself as one of the best young pitching prospects on the island.

Ramon learned his major-league pitching technique at Campos Las Palmas.

★ 3 ★

TO THE OLYMPICS

Avila followed Ramon's progress closely. As manager of the country's Olympic baseball team, Avila selected Ramon to pitch in the 1984 Olympics in Los Angeles. It was an incredible experience. When Ramon took the mound at Dodgers Stadium, he felt right at home. He even predicted that he would be back someday. He told a Dodgers scout: "Maybe in four years, I'll be back here pitching."

Ramon pitched three scoreless innings against Taiwan and impressed the Dodgers scouts with his tremendous confidence. They were a little worried about his slender build, but Avila

Ramon signed with the Dodgers after his impressive
performance at the 1984 Olympics.

assured them that once Ramon put on a little weight, he would be a top pitcher. The Dodgers trusted Avila—he knew Dominican baseball better than anyone.

Three weeks after the Olympics, the Dodgers offered Ramon a contract. It was everything he had ever dreamed about, but it would mean moving to a new country, learning a new language, and leaving school. Ramon decided it was worth the gamble

Ramon's prediction that he would play for the Dodgers proved correct.

because he believed he could make it to the major leagues. He accepted the offer. Seven months later Ramon found himself in Bradenton, Florida, the first stop on his way to the big leagues.

★ 4 ★

EATING FOR HIS LIFE

Ramon Martinez was worried about what he would face in the minor leagues. He had just turned 17, and he was afraid of being isolated and alone. Luckily, the Dodgers had many Spanish-speaking players in their system. In fact, more than a dozen of his teammates came from the Caribbean or South America. They helped and supported each other both on and off the field.

Ramon pitched mainly in middle relief in 1985. In 1986, he was sent to the Dodgers' minor-league club in Bakersfield, California, where he learned to throw a proper change-up from coach Johnny Podres. "He told me I had a great fastball

Ramon's new pitch fooled most minor-league hitters.

Ramon was simply too skinny to pitch full games.

and this would only make it better," Ramon says. "He showed me how to hold the ball with a different grip and how to throw it. I learned right away. It worked from the very beginning."

Ramon's new pitch helped get him into the starting rotation. Yet it was here that he encountered his first major setback. California League hitters were patient. They made Ramon work deep into the count, waiting for him to make a mistake and throw his fastball over the plate. Ramon gave up a lot of hits and runs, and lost many games he should have won.

Of greater concern to the Dodgers was that their young star often ran out of energy after four or five innings. Ramon had the ability to be a great starter, but at 6' 3" and 135 pounds, he was too frail to hold up for an entire season. "When I was in the clubhouse I used to look at other people and see how skinny I was and feel real bad," he remembers.

As bad as Ramon felt, his old friend Ralph Avila felt even worse. When Ramon returned to the Dominican Republic that winter, Avila could hardly believe his eyes. Ramon was not only failing to gain weight as he matured—he was actually *losing* weight! Avila forbid him to play baseball and put him on a special diet, which included vitamins and high-protein milkshakes. He arranged unlimited credit for Ramon at a local cafeteria and instructed Ramon to eat as if his life depended on it.

Although it nearly drove him crazy through the winter, Ramon packed on 17 important pounds. When he arrived at spring training in 1987, he was bigger, stronger, and well rested. On his first day of camp, Ramon suited up, took the mound, reared back and fired a fastball that exploded into the catcher's mitt. When Dodgers coaches put the radar gun on Ramon, they had to rub their eyes to make sure they were not seeing things. His fastball registered over 90 miles per hour—10 miles per hour faster than the season before!

Heavier and well rested, Ramon had reason to smile when he returned to spring training in 1987.

Ramon quickly blossomed into the Dodger organization's top young pitcher. He won 16 games in 1987 and gave up just 41 earned runs in 25 starts.

In 1988, Ramon blew through the minor leagues. Meanwhile, at the major-league level, the Dodgers were struggling to keep their pitching rotation together. When pitching injuries threatened the team's first-place lead, the coaches decided to call up Ramon. It was very risky to throw a 20-year-old rookie into the pressure of a pennant race, but the Dodgers had no choice. They handed Ramon the ball in a key game against the Montreal Expos.

Ramon responded magnificently, mowing down Montreal's sluggers and keeping his cool when the Expo speedsters reached base. He left the game after seven innings, credited with a 2–1 victory. As tempting as it was for the Dodgers to keep Ramon in the majors, they knew it was

SAN ANTONIO '88
MISSIONS

RAMON MARTINEZ P

Ramon began 1988 in San Antonio, where he won eight games.

In his major league debut, Ramon pitched seven impressive innings against the Expos.

smarter to bring him along slowly. He spent most of 1989 at the Triple-A level, where he went 10–2 with 127 strikeouts in 113 innings.

When a series of extra-inning games pushed the Los Angeles starting rotation to its limits, Ramon filled in for one start against the Atlanta Braves. He gave the fans a preview of things to come by pitching a six-hit shutout. Five weeks later, he returned to the majors for good and finished the year with six wins.

★ 5 ★

THE MAJOR LEAGUES

Ramon Martinez finally became a member of the Dodgers starting rotation in 1990. He responded with one of the greatest pitching seasons in the last 20 years. He became an instant sensation on June 4, when he pitched a 6–0 shutout against the Atlanta Braves, and struck out 18 batters. The only other Dodger to accomplish this feat was Hall of Famer Sandy Koufax. He watched Ramon on television and called to congratulate him after the game. "That was a huge experience in my life," says Ramon. "It was one of the principal factors in opening the doors to the major leagues for me, because, although I had started here the year before,

Ramon tips his cap after striking out 18 Atlanta Braves on
June 4, 1990.

By the end of 1990, Ramon had won 20 games.

I still wasn't very well known. But after I tied Sandy Koufax's record with those 18 strikeouts, I began to be recognized."

Ramon continued his magnificent run and finished with a 20–6 record. He led the National League with 12 complete games and became the youngest 20-game winner in team history.

Ramon followed his red-hot 1990 season with another good performance in 1991. But a lot of innings—and a tremendous amount of responsibility—had been heaped upon his young arm. Toward the end of the year, the wear and

Ramon rests during a break.

tear began to show. Although his record was a respectable 17–13, his fastball seemed to have less movement and he could not strike out batters as easily as he had the year before. In 1992, Ramon had a terrible season. He won only eight games and gave up four earned runs a game. The same people who had proclaimed him a future Hall of Famer were now calling him a "flash in the pan."

Ramon's arm was aching and his pride was wounded, too. "I never had that kind of year," he says. "It was frustrating. I felt the pain in August and decided to stop. I had pitched with pain before, but not this bad."

Ramon worked on his delivery that winter in order to reduce the stress on his body. As it turned out, he pitched a little better in 1993, but he suffered control problems for the first time in his career. Then, in 1994, Ramon regained full command of his pitches. His record stood at 12–7 when the season was cut short by a labor dispute.

Ramon keeps an eye on a runner at first base.

Naturally, everyone was expecting a big year from Ramon in 1995, but instead of taking another step forward, he seemed to take a step back. At the end of June, he had allowed more walks and earned runs than anyone in the league. He hit rock bottom in a July 2 game against the San Diego Padres, when the Dodger Stadium fans booed him off the mound. That had never happened to Ramon in his life.

Then, when things looked their worst, something extraordinary happened. Prior to Ramon's July 14 start against the Florida Marlins, he had a brief meeting in the team's video room with manager Tom Lasorda, pitching coach Dave Wallace, and Ralph Avila. Whatever they discussed did wonders for Ramon, who had his extra-good stuff right from the first pitch. Without giving up a single hit, Ramon retired one batter after another. In the ninth inning, the crowd was going crazy. "I was trying to concentrate on my game," says Ramon, who knew that one bad pitch could cost him his no-hitter. "I said, 'Don't change anything. Don't try to overthrow.'"

Ramon struck out slugger Charles Johnson and got Jerry Browne to bounce out to second

Ramon reacts to the last out of his no-hitter.

base. Then, he held his breath as the pesky
Quilvio Veras fouled off several pitches before
lofting an easy fly ball for the final out.
A wide grin spread across his face as he was
mobbed on the same mound where he had heard
boos just a few days before.

Ramon is mobbed by excited teammates and coaches.

Ramon speaks to the press after the no-hitter.

"It was a great feeling," says Ramon, who wanted to share his joy with everyone. "For many people—the guys, my fans and my family—I was very excited. Everyone was going crazy, especially people back home. I have pride and I wanted to let people know that I can still pitch. You know something? I think people had forgotten about me!"

Ramon lost just one more game that year. He reestablished himself as the ace of the Los Angeles rotation, and helped the Dodgers win the division title.

In 1996, Ramon turned in another fine performance despite a painful groin injury. He finished with a flurry, winning his final seven decisions. He also got his 100th career victory and struck out his 1,000th batter. The highlight of the season, however, was the August 29 game against the Montreal Expos, when Ramon faced his younger brother, Pedro. In a tight, well-played ballgame, Ramon allowed just three infield singles, while Pedro struck out a career-high 12 batters. The Dodgers won 2–1 on back-to-back home runs by Mike Piazza and Eric Karros. It was a shame that only one brother could win.

Ramon is now at the mid-point of his career. He already ranks among the greatest hurlers in the history of the Los Angeles Dodgers, and he is one of the most feared right-handers in baseball.

Ramon's brother, Pedro Martinez

Before Pedro joined the Expos, the Martinez brothers played togther on the Dodgers.

What lies ahead for Ramon?

Many believe he can win another 100 games before he hangs up his spikes. They say he has both the talent and the experience to do what it takes. Ramon's goals, however, are a little simpler. "I just want to keep pitching the way I have," he says. "I don't worry about what's ahead. . . . I know it'll be very tough to keep going the same way—I know I'll have to work very hard. So that's what I'll do."

Ramon knows he must work hard to keep pitching well.

C ★ H ★ R ★ O ★ N

1968 • Ramon Martinez is born in Santo Domingo, Dominican Republic.

1984 • Ramon impresses Dodgers scouts when he pitches for the Dominican Republic in the Olympics.

1987 • Ramon wins 16 games for Vero Beach of the Florida State League.

1988 • After being called up to the major leagues by the Dodgers, Ramon beats the Montreal Expos 2–1 in his first start.

O ☆ L ☆ O ☆ G ☆ Y

1990   • In Ramon's first full season in the major leagues, he wins 20 games and makes the All-Star team.

1994   • Ramon ties for the N.L. lead with three shutouts.

1995   • Ramon throws a no-hitter against the Florida Marlins on July 14.

1996   • For the second consecutive year, Ramon leads the Dodgers to the playoffs.

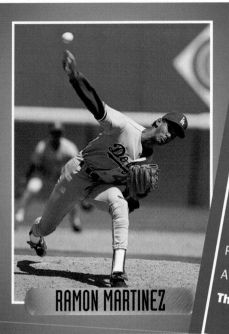

RAMON MARTINEZ

RAMON MARTINEZ

Place of Birth **Santo Domingo, Dominican Republic**

Date of Birth **March 22, 1968**

Height **6' 4"**

Weight **186 pounds**

High School **Liceo Secunderia Las Americas**

Pro Team **Los Angeles Dodgers**

All-Star **1990, 1991**

Threw no-hitter **July 14, 1995**

MAJOR LEAGUE STATISTICS

Season	Team	W	L	Pct.	ERA	G	IP	H	SO
1988	Los Angeles	1	3	.250	3.78	9	35	27	23
1989	Los Angeles	6	4	.600	3.19	15	98	79	89
1990	Los Angeles	20	6	.769	2.92	33	234	191	223
1991	Los Angeles	17	13	.567	3.27	33	220	190	150
1992	Los Angeles	8	11	.421	4.00	25	150	141	101
1993	Los Angeles	10	12	.455	3.44	32	211	202	127
1994	Los Angeles	12	7	.632	3.97	24	170	160	119
1995	Los Angeles	17	7	.708	3.66	30	206	176	138
1996	Los Angeles	15	6	.714	3.44	27	168	153	132
Totals		**106**	**69**	**.610**	**3.51**	**228**	**1502**	**1319**	**1102**

--- ★ ★ ★ ---

ABOUT THE AUTHOR

Mark Stewart grew up in New York City in the
1960s and 1970s–when the Mets, Jets, and
Knicks all had championship teams. As a child,
Mark read everything about sports he could lay
his hands on. Today, he is one of the busiest
sportswriters around. Since 1990, he has written
close to 500 sports stories for kids, including
profiles on more than 200 atheletes, past and
present. A graduate of Duke University, Mark
served as senior editor of *Racquet,* a national
tennis magazine, and was managing editor of
Super News, a sporting goods industry
newspaper. He is the author of every Grolier
All-Pro Biography and four titles in the
Children's Press Sports Stars series.